If You Played Hide-and-Seek with a Chameleon

By Bill Wise ⌢◆⌢ Illustrated by Rebecca Evans

Dawn Publications

To Ellie, Love Papa. — B.W.

For Matthew Stewart. I can only do what I love because you love me enough
to make it possible. Thank you. — R.E.

Acknowledgment

The publisher wishes to thank zookeeper Dave Johnson for vetting
the factual content of this book.

Library of Congress Cataloging-in-Publication Data

Names: Wise, Bill, 1958- author. | Evans, Rebecca, illustrator.

Title: If you played hide-and-seek with a chameleon / by Bill Wise ;
  illustrated by Rebecca Evans.

Description: First edition. | Nevada City, CA : Dawn Publications, [2019] |
  Audience: Ages 5-11. | Audience: K to grade 3.

Identifiers: LCCN 2018046404| ISBN 9781584696506 (hardcover) | ISBN
  9781584696513 (pbk.)

Subjects: LCSH: Adaptation (Biology)--Juvenile literature. |
  Animals--Miscellanea--Juvenile literature.

Classification: LCC QH546 .W57 2019 | DDC 591.4--dc23 LC record
available at https://lccn.loc.gov/2018046404

Book design and computer production by
Patty Arnold, *Menagerie Design and Publishing*
Cover title font: Duality
Interior story font: Pink Martini
Illustrations: Watercolor

Manufactured by Regent Publishing Services, Hong Kong
Printed July, 2019, in ShenZhen, Guangdong, China
10 9 8 7 6 5 4 3 2 1
First Edition

Dawn Publications

12402 Bitney Springs Road
Nevada City, CA 95959
800-545-7475
www.dawnpub.com

If you played games with animals, would you win or lose?

If you entered a pie-eating contest
with a hippo, you'd lose.

A hippo has the biggest mouth of all land animals. It eats about 100 pounds of food every night. That's like eating more than 50 pies — but the pies would need to be made out of grass, a hippo's favorite food. How many pies can you eat in one night?

If you played hide-and-seek with a chameleon, you'd lose.

A chameleon is a master of disguise! You could be looking directly at a chameleon and not even know it's there. And you can forget about finding a good spot to hide from a chameleon. It can move its eyes separately to see in two different directions at the same time.

If you played basketball with a giraffe, you'd lose.

An adult giraffe towers over an official basketball hoop. It could easily block every shot you tried. Even if you stood on a step ladder, you still wouldn't be able to sink a basket or stop a giraffe from dunking the ball.

If you competed in a long-jumping event
with a kangaroo, you'd lose.

A kangaroo's body is made for jumping. Its strong back legs and huge feet give it lots of power. A kangaroo can leap from one end of a classroom to the other in a single hop. How many hops would it take you?

If you competed in a weight lifting contest with an elephant, you'd lose.

An elephant can carry the weight of about 120 grown-ups. Can you carry even one grown-up? You and 200 of your friends together couldn't haul as much weight as one elephant can.

If you wrestled with an anaconda, you'd lose.

An anaconda weighs about as much as you and eleven of your friends combined. You don't want to risk getting caught in a headlock by this big reptile — an anaconda squeezes its prey until the prey stops breathing. Maybe just give him some lemons to squeeze.

FRESH
ANACONDA SQUEEZED
LEMONADE

If you raced a cheetah, you'd lose.

A cheetah is the fastest animal on land. While riding in a car on the highway, you could look out your window and see a cheetah keeping up with you. In a 100-meter dash, you'd just be passing the 30-meter mark as the cheetah was crossing the finish line.

If you played Twister
with an octopus, you'd lose.

An octopus is super flexible because it doesn't have any bones.
With its eight arms—each equipped with suction cups—an
octopus could cover twice as many circles on the Twister mat.

If you played tag with a porcupine,
you'd lose.

A porcupine has 30,000 quills on its body. As soon as you tagged it, dozens of these quills would detach and plunge into your skin. Do you really want to feel like a human pincushion?

If you competed in a staring contest
with a shark, you'd lose.

A shark never shuts its eyes. It can't.
It doesn't have eyelids. It's impossible for a shark to blink.
But humans blink about 1–20 times per minute.
You have the same chance of beating a shark
in a staring contest as the shark has of beating
you in a game of Go Fish.

If you played Blind Potato Race
with a bat, you'd lose.

The challenge of a potato race is
trying to find the most potatoes
when you can't see them. But wearing a
blindfold wouldn't hinder a bat. It makes high-
pitched sounds and then listens for the echoes that bounce
back from objects. In this way, it "sees" with its ears. A bat could find
all the potatoes while you stumble around.

If you played tennis with a snail . . . well, you'd win that game!

It takes a snail about one minute to move one yard (almost a meter).
Unless you hit the ball directly at the snail, it wouldn't be able to
move fast enough to return your shot.

But a snail is an expert at making a slime trail.
Can you do THAT?

Fun Facts and Fascinating Feats

The animals in the story are shown playing games and doing things they could never do. But the explanations on each page are accurate. Discover more fun facts and fascinating feats about these amazing animals.

A **hippo** has a big mouth, but it can go three weeks without eating if it can't find food. When a hippo dives underwater, it's nostrils close tightly—no water up its nose! Male hippos impress females by flinging their dung (poop) with their tails.

A **chameleon** shoots out its tongue like a rocket—so fast it can catch a fly in midair. The spit at the end acts like glue to hold the prey. Then it reels its tongue back into its mouth like sucking in a strand of spaghetti.

A **giraffe** is the tallest land animal on Earth—about the height of a two-story building. It can grab and eat the leaves that other animals can't reach. It's super long tongue is dark to keep it from getting sunburned.

An **elephant** has thick skin, but it's very sensitive. To prevent sunburns, an elephant covers its skin with dust or mud. Its trunk is powerful enough to carry a calf and precise enough to pick a flower.

A **kangaroo** can jump 25 feet (7.6 meters) in a single hop. But it can't hop backwards. Males are expert fighters. They jab like a boxer and kick like a martial artist. A baby kangaroo is about the size of a cherry when it's born.

An **anaconda** doesn't have venom, but it is deadly. It suffocates its prey by squeezing it and then stretches its mouth wide enough to swallow the prey whole — even animals as big as wild pigs and deer.

A **cheetah** actually spends more time sleeping than running. When it does sprint, its long tail acts like a rudder keeping it steady. A cheetah can't roar. But it can purr, similar to a house cat.

An **octopus** can untie knots and open jars. It defends itself by squeezing into a shell, squirting a cloud of ink, or changing color and texture to camouflage itself. A Giant Pacific Octopus is as long as a school bus.

A **porcupine** can't see well and moves slowly. It would be easy prey except for one thing—its quills. Some people think a porcupine shoots it quills at a predator. It doesn't. The quills come off when touched.

A **shark** doesn't have any bones. Its skeleton is made of cartilage— the same tissue human ears are made of. Sharks continually shed their teeth. But backup teeth move in to replace any they lose. One species loses 35,000 teeth in its lifetime.

A **bat** is the only mammal that can truly fly. If you compare a bat skeleton with a human skeleton, you'll see that the bones in its wing are like the fingers of a hand. It hangs upside down by its thumbs. Bats are not blind, but many species rely on echolocation to find food.

A **snail** leaves a tell-tale trail of sticky slime (mucus) wherever it goes. The slime allows the snail to climb up a wall or travel upside down. Its eyes are at the end of two tentacles on top of its head.

Take a Closer Look

There's a snail hidden in every illustration. Look closely and you may find every one of them.

More things to discover:

 There are five friends entering the animal fair. They're together in all of the illustrations except for two. Which illustration shows only four of them? Which shows only three?

 Five chameleons are hiding in the Fun House. Can you find them all?

Every illustration features an animal playing a game. Find that animal on the *following* page. It may be wearing a blue ribbon.

 Every illustration also shows the animal that will be featured playing a game on the *next* page. Can you find it? For example, the hippo is selling tickets on the first page, and it's the animal in the pie-eating contest on the next page.

In the final illustration, five animals are shown celebrating with the kids. Which ones are missing? Why do you think they aren't shown?

Need a hint?
Go to http://tinyurl.com/ifyouplayed.

Science, Technology, Engineering, Math

This book uses a fun, imaginative approach to combine science, sports, and math. It can be used to spark children's interest in an individual subject or as an introduction to an interdisciplinary unit. Use the STEM suggestions below as a springboard for your own creativity, adjusting them for younger or older children.

Science

Habitat Happenings—Divide students into 12 small groups and assign each group one of the animals from the story to investigate. Have students identify where the animal lives and the characteristics of its habitat (plants, animals, climate). Using craft materials, have students show their findings by creating a diorama or food chain mobile.

More Games to Play—Have students create an additional page for the book. Begin by having them choose an animal and identify a game or sport the animal would play. Explain that their page should follow the book's format to include (1) an illustration, (2) a sentence with the animal's name and the game it's playing, and (3) a few sentences describing the animal's amazing ability, along with an explanation about why a child would lose the competition to the animal.

Technology

Computer Graphs—Have students use a computer to create a bar graph. Suggest to children that the graph's horizontal axis should be labeled "Number of legs" with the number of legs (0 legs, 2 legs, 4 legs, 5 legs, 8 legs) written below where the bars will be drawn. The vertical axis should be labeled "Number of animals" with intervals of 1, from 1 through 10. Older students may create a histogram instead of a bar graph.

Engineering

I Want a Rematch—Engineers solve problems. Give students an engineering design challenge to create an invention that would help them win if they competed against one of the animals in the book. For example, a pair of multi-view glasses might help them win a game of hide-and-seek with a chameleon or protective gloves could help them play tag with a porcupine.

Math

Weights and Lengths—Choose 12 students and give each one a bookmark of a different animal. Without talking, have them arrange themselves in order by weight, from lightest (garden snail) to heaviest (African elephant). Then read the actual weight of each animal. Some children may have to change their position to create the correct order.

Pulling Your Leg—Write the number of legs for each of the 12 animals on the board. (Scientists say that a snail has one foot, but no legs. And, surprisingly, research concludes that a kangaroo has five legs because its tail acts like a leg when a kangaroo is walking.) Use the legs for math problems. The examples below range from grades 1st through 5th.

- Add the number of legs of two animals (example: hippo and giraffe is $4 + 4 = 8$) or three animals (example: hippo, snake, and snail is $4 + 0 + 0 = 4$). It can be fun for children to choose the animals.

- Add the total number of legs for all 12 animals. (answer: 39)

- Create subtraction problems using the number of legs (example: elephant minus a bat is $4 - 2 = 2$).

- Ask children what fraction of the animals have 0 legs; 2 legs; 4 legs; and 8 legs.

- Have children find the percent equivalent for each fraction. You may let them use a calculator.

What's the Word—Create word problems for older students using the Table of Measurements.

⚑ Choose two animals and have students find the animals' total weight and their total length and/or height.

⚑ Choose two animals and have students determine how much heavier one animal is than the other. (Subtract the lesser weight from the greater weight.) Then have students determine how much longer one animal is than the other. (Subtract the lesser length from the greater length.)

⚑ Choose three animals and calculate how much heavier or lighter each animal is compared to an adult (either male or female).

⚑ Choose the heaviest animal and calculate how many times heavier this animal is than an adult. Then choose the lightest animal and calculate how many times heavier an adult is than this animal.

⚑ Choose the tallest animal and calculate how many times taller it is than a human. Then choose the smallest animal and calculate how many times bigger a human is than this animal.

Table of Measurements

Standard (Customary) Units of Measure

	Weight	Length	Height
Hippo	5000 lb	11 ft	5 ft
Indian Chameleon	.4 lb (6.4 oz)	1 ft (12 in)	N/A
Giraffe	2500 lb	4.75 ft	15 ft
Red Kangaroo	200 lb	6 ft.	5 ft
African Elephant	10000 lb	20 ft	11 ft
Green Anaconda	330 lb	22 ft	N/A
Cheetah	125 lb	4 ft	2.5 ft (2 ft 6 in)
Giant Pacific Octopus	110 lb	16 ft	N/A
N. American Porcupine	25 lb	2.5 ft (2 ft 6 in)	N/A
Great White Shark	4200 lb	16 ft	N/A
Long-eared Bat	.02 lb (.32 oz)	.25 ft (3 in)	wing span .83 ft (10 in)
Garden Snail	.05 lb (.8 oz)	.1 ft (1.2 in)	N/A
Human—adult male (North America)	199 lb	N/A	5 ft 9 in
Human—adult female (North America)	171 lb	N/A	5 ft 4 in

Metric Units of Measure

	Weight	Length	Height
Hippo	2268 kg	3.4 m	1.5 m
Indian Chameleon	.17 kg	.3 m (30 cm)	N/A
Giraffe	1134 kg	1.5 m	4.6 m
Red Kangaroo	91kg	2.5 m	1.5 m
African Elephant	4536 kg	6.1 m	3.3 m
Green Anaconda	150 kg	6.7 m	N/A
Cheetah	57 kg	1.2 m	.8 m
Giant Pacific Octopus	50 kg	4.9 m	N/A
N. American Porcupine	11 kg	.8 m	N/A
Great White Shark	1950 kg	4.9 m	N/A
Long-eared Bat	.01 kg	.045 m (4.5 cm)	wing span .25 m (25cm)
Garden Snail	.02 kg	.03 m (3 cm)	N/A
Human—adult male (North America)	90.4 kg	N/A	1.8 m
Human—adult female (North America)	77.4 kg	N/A	1.7 m

Note: The above measurements are an average for each species of animal portrayed in the book. Metric measurements are rounded to the nearest whole number or decimal. For measurements of adults from a specific country or a different continent go to www.worlddata.info/average-bodyheight.php.

The Table of Measurements is available as free download. Also available are additional resources, including bookmarks of the animals, a writing lesson plan, and suggestions for reading the book aloud. Go to www.dawnpub.com/activities/if-you-played-hide-and-seek-with-a-chameleon.

Bill Wise is a retired middle school teacher who now writes full-time. In addition to teaching math and English, he coached baseball and basketball (his favorite sport) for many years. This book was inspired by Bill's passion for sports, nature, and mathematics. As a former teacher he likes to create activities that connect math with nature and sports. Bill has written five children's books. His picture book biography *Louis Sockalexis: Native American Baseball Pioneer* earned the International Reading Association's primary nonfiction book award. He lives in Maine with his wife, Mary Ann. Visit him at bwiseauthor.com.

Rebecca Evans started drawing as soon as she could hold a crayon and just never stopped. After working for nine years as an artist and designer, she returned to her first love—children's book illustration. She's authored and/or illustrated nineteen books. She also teaches art in local art programs and is a Co-Regional Advisor for SCBWI. Rebecca currently lives in Maryland and enjoys spending time with her husband and four young children, while working from her home studio during every spare moment. Find her at http://rebeccaevans.net.

Also Illustrated by Rebecca Evans

Why Should I Walk? I Can Fly!—A little bird, a big sky, and the first time out of the nest! A robin's first flight is a gentle reminder about what we can accomplish if we just keep trying.

More Nature Appreciation Books From Dawn Publications

Scampers Thinks Like a Scientist—Scampers is no ordinary mouse—she knows how to investigate. Her infectiously experimental spirit will have young readers eager to think like scientists, too!

There's a Bug on My Book—All sorts of critters that hop, fly, wiggle, and slide across the pages of this book, engaging children's imaginations while introducing them to the animals in the grass beneath their feet.

Pass the Energy, Please!—Everyone is somebody's lunch. In this upbeat rhyming story, the food chain connects herbivores, carnivores, insects, and plants together in a fascinating circle of players.

How We Know What We Know About Our Changing Climate—Discover the science behind the headlines with evidence from nature gathered by scientists from all over the world. For upper elementary and middle school.

Daytime Nighttime, All Through the Year—Delightful rhymes and unique illustrations depict two animals for each month of the year, one active during the day and one busy at night.

Octopus Escapes Again!—Swim along with Octopus as she searches for food and outwits dangerous enemies by using a dazzling display of defenses. Oh yes, Octopus escapes again and again!

Wonderful Nature, Wonderful You—Nature can be a great teacher. With a light touch especially suited to children, this 20th anniversary edition evokes feelings of calm acceptance, joy, and wonder.

Earth Heroes: Champions of Wild Animals—A collection of biographies of men and women who played a role in saving whole species of animals. For upper elementary and middle school.

Dawn Publications is dedicated to inspiring in children a deeper understanding and appreciation for all life on Earth. You can browse through our titles, download resources for teachers, and order at www.dawnpub.com or call 800-545-7475.